Ralphie and His Race

Written By Marion Brooks

Published By Linden-Wolf LLC

Ralphie and His Race

ISBN: 978-1-7375886-0-3

Today is the annual potato sack race. It's a super exciting event! Everyone in town is sure to attend.

Last year, Ralphie and his teddy bear BB came in first place.

They won a trophy so big, that both he and BB could fit inside of it!

Ralphie feels confident about hopping in this race.

Every day after school, Ralphie would practice by hopping all the way home as fast as he could.

Ralphie's dad has been competing in the annual race since he was a little boy. Out of every race, he only lost one time.

Ralphie hopes to carry on the tradition by winning today's race.

From the sideline, Ralphie's dad yells, " Stay focused on the race and don't turn around while you are hopping!"

"On your mark! Get Set! Go!" yells the referee.

Ralphie quickly hops to the front of the pack. Suddenly, he notices someone coming up behind him.

Ralphie panics and turns around to see who it is.

The crowd screams loudly as Alex hops passed the finish line to win the race.

Ralphie is upset because he and BB lost the race.
"I can't believe we lost!" cries Ralphie.
"We practiced extremely hard for this race!"

"Ralphie, what's wrong?" asks Ralphie's dad.

"We didn't come in first place and now we just want to go home!" Ralphie answers sadly.

"Remember, Ralphie, I have also lost before. I lost my very first race. I practiced with my best friend Michael and when the race began,
I was faster than everyone else, just like you!"
"I was so excited to be in the lead, that I looked back to see how far I was in front of everyone."

"That was my biggest mistake. I broke my concentration and slowed down. Michale took the lead and won the race - fair and square. He practiced just as hard as I did, so I said, Congratulations!"

"You're right," Ralphie says as he gives his father a hug.

Ralphie slowly drags BB over to Alex to congratulate him on winning the race.

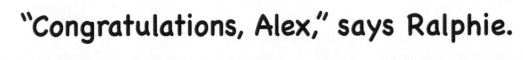

"Congratulations, Alex," says Ralphie.

"Thank you," says Alex. "You really are a fast, potato sack hopper, Ralphie. Do you want to be on my team for the next race?" asks Alex.

"Thanks, Alex! I would love to be on your team!" beams Ralphie.

"Good job," says Ralphie's dad.

On your mark, get set, GO!!!

How do **YOU** react when you lose at something?

DEDICATION

" For the hands that helped shape my
character. Majorie and Pearlena"

"Family is everything"

CPSIA information can be obtained
at www.ICGtesting.com
Printed in the USA
BVRC101252070821
613916BV00009B/17